Also by Val Wilding

Toby Tucker: Keeping Sneaky Secrets
Toby Tucker: Sludging through a Sewer
Toby Tucker: Mucking about with Monkeys
Toby Tucker: Picking People's Pockets
Toby Tucker: Hogging all the Pig Swill

TOBY TUCKER

Dodging the Donkey Doo

VAL WILDING

Illustrated by Michael Broad

EGMONT

For my dear friend Maggie, with love

EGMONT
We bring stories to life

Published in Great Britain 2007
by Egmont UK Limited
239 Kensington High Street, London W8 6SA

Text copyright © 2007 Val Wilding
Illustrations copyright © 2007 Michael Broad

The moral rights of the author and illustrator have been asserted

ISBN 978 1 4052 2547 2

1 3 5 7 9 10 8 6 4 2

A CIP catalogue record for this title is available
from the British Library

Printed and bound in Great Britain by the CPI Group

The Allen house, present day

Toby Tucker kicked the front door shut behind him.

His startled foster parents, Don and Evie Allen, appeared in the kitchen doorway, both clutching paintbrushes. Don's nose was blue, and Evie's hair was dappled with pale yellow paint.

'Good job we haven't decorated the front door yet,' said Don.

'Sorry,' said Toby. 'Had a rotten day.'

Evie ran the tap to wash her hands. 'Let's all have a cuppa, and you can tell us what's wrong.'

'We had PE,' Toby grumbled. 'I hate it. We did the first trials for sports day, and it's no good – I just can't run. I'm always last.'

1

Evie said, 'Don will go running with you if you want to practise. Won't you, Don?'

Behind Toby's back, Don made a face.

'Thanks, but no thanks,' said Toby. 'It won't do any good. Not even worth trying.'

Don blew his cheeks out in relief. 'Tell you what, lad. I've got something in the basement to show you. I was going to surprise you at the weekend but –'

'Oh no, you don't!' said Evie. 'Once you get down in your playroom I won't see you till bed-time!'

Toby giggled.

'It is not my playroom,' said Don huffily. 'It's a games room.'

'I don't care if it's World of Big Boys Toyserama Are Us,' said Evie. 'Toby, homework first, then dinner and afterwards you can do exactly as you want. And you,' she said, shoving a paintbrush in Don's hand, 'ceiling. Now!'

Toby grinned at Don, grabbed a chocolate

2

wafer and scooted upstairs to the very top of the house. He went in his warm, bright room, closed the door and looked round. His own room. If things went OK here, he'd never have to share with other boys in a children's home ever again.

He was happy here. He could forget rotten PE and just be himself, Toby Tucker. No friends had ever been up here, and weren't likely to – not until the pink fairy wallpaper went. Don and Evie still had a lot of repairs and decorating to do before they got up as far as here. Toby didn't mind. He didn't want anyone up here. Not until he'd got used to the wooden chest.

He whizzed through his homework – maths, which was a doddle – then crossed to the window. The chest stood on the floor, looking totally innocent.

But it held a secret. A secret so enormous and so strange that Toby hadn't yet found a way to tell Don and Evie. They were the closest thing he had to a family, but he'd only lived with them for three weeks.

Toby knelt and opened the chest. He took out a framed photo of an elderly man with a gentle face. The warm feeling that Toby always got when he looked at the photo flooded over him. He turned it over and read, again, the pencilled note on the back.

The paper in the chest is your family tree. I wonder which little baby tore it up, eh, Toby Tucker? Piece it together and you'll find out who you are and when you come from.

Gee.

Toby chuckled. 'When you come from!'

The first time he'd read it, he thought Gee, whoever he was, had got it

4.

wrong – that he meant to write 'where you come from'.

But now Toby knew differently. Inside the chest were piles of torn paper, all with scraps of writing on. He'd learned the secret of the chest when he'd manage to piece together the name 'Seti'. The result was the most incredible thing that had ever happened to him. Toby had actually become Seti for a while. He'd lived in a farm on the banks of the River Nile in Ancient Egypt!

Toby yearned to piece together another name, and he'd been trying ever since. Would it, could it, happen again? He pulled out a handful of scraps and read them aloud. 'Wil, ita, Egb, nius . . .' None of those seemed to fit together.

He kicked off his shoes and put a CD on. After dinner, he promised himself, he'd settle down and see if he could finally put together another piece in the puzzle that was his family tree.

Don yelled up the stairs. 'Toby! Supper's

ready! Steak pie, mash, carrots, courgettes and Evie's special glue – I mean gravy!'

Toby grinned. Evie would get her own back for that! She didn't mind. She was a great cook, and she knew it.

Having dinner together was important in the Allen household. They shared their news, jokes, gossip and problems and it was at these times that Toby felt he almost belonged here. Almost.

But if he didn't belong here, he wondered, where did he belong? Nobody knew anything of his past. That's why it was so vital that he pieced together his family tree, to find out the answer to the question they all asked.

Who's Toby Tucker?

'Dearest, darling Evie, best cook in the world, kindest and brainiest –'

'Most generous and beautiful,' added Toby.

'Sweetest and –'

Evie laughed. 'Oh, go on, then, I'll clear up.

Go down to your playroom!'

The games room was once the cellar, and Toby went carefully down the steep, narrow steps. Inside, the room was surprisingly large.

'Wow!' said Toby. 'Table tennis!'

'Got it at an auction,' said Don. 'I'd rather have a snooker table, but they're too expensive. Come on. I haven't played for years.' He handed

Toby a bat.

Ten minutes later, Toby picked the ball up from where Don had smashed it into a corner. 'That's it,' he said. 'I've had enough. I'm useless at this as well.'

'Have another game,' suggested Don. 'You'll improve. I expect you're just rusty.'

'You're not rusty, and you haven't played for years.' Toby climbed the stairs. 'See you later.'

He went straight to his room and plonked down on the floor. He was very fed up. I'm no good at anything, he thought.

Toby found, to his surprise, that he was still holding the bat and ball. Crossly, he batted the ball against the wall, aiming at a lavender fairy's head. He missed.

'Can't even hit that,' he moaned, and

8

bashed the ball against the wall over and over, missing the fairy's head every time. He gave the ball an extra hard whack. It hit the wall and shot back over his head, bounced off the cupboard behind him and ricocheted round the room, coming to rest by the chest.

He'd almost forgotten his plan to have another go at the family tree tonight!

Toby put on his favourite CD. He opened the chest, took out armfuls of paper and sat in the middle of the deep red carpet. He spread the scraps out and began to sort through them. He decided on a strategy. He'd choose one piece, then try every other piece until he found a match. It could take days, but at least he'd end up with a name.

And a name, he believed, was all he needed for the chest to reveal its secret once more.

Toby closed his eyes, riffled through the pile and selected a piece of paper. Opening his eyes, he read, 'leon'.

Leon's a name by itself, he thought, and laid the paper on the carpet. He waited. Nothing.

'Toby Tucker, where are your brains?' he said. 'Names begin with a capital letter. That means there's a bit missing from the front of this one.'

He began trying to match other scraps of paper to 'leon'.

'Elizaleon? No. Judileon? Doubt it. Leleon? Not likely. Nikoleon? Never heard of that na–'

Toby froze. A small drawing of a boy was appearing beside 'Nikoleon'. A boy in a short tunic and tatty sandals.

As he stared, his tummy churning with excitement, the drawing changed. It morphed into a drawing of himself – Toby Tucker! Then just as quickly it changed back. As it did so, it shimmered. The shimmer grew and grew, and when it was half as high as the room, the silvery light moved towards Toby, and passed right over him. He got the same feeling he'd had before – the feeling of cold, wobbly jelly sliding through his whole body.

Toby turned, almost sure of what he would see. Yes! There was the boy – the boy in the tunic! – standing with his back to the room, right where the chest should be.

Taking a deep breath, Toby walked towards the boy. As he did so, two things happened. He felt himself being pulled forward, as if by a huge magnet, and he tripped over the table tennis bat.

The room was spinning. Everything in it was a blur as Toby cried, 'Look out!'

He tumbled head first into the boy. 'Ooof!' he cried as his head thumped into something warm and soft. Then he felt a tearing pain in the side of his head, as if his hair was being yanked out by the roots. 'Yeeow!'

He saw stars for a moment. 'What's happened?' he said. 'I can't remember . . . Who am I?'

He shook his head to clear it. 'Of course,' he muttered. 'I'm me. Nikoleon. And my feet are covered in donkey doo.'

430 BC, near Athens, Greece

It's hardly a good idea to head-butt a donkey, and
I'll never know what made me do it this morning.
One minute I was standing there wondering
which of the stubborn creatures to take to market,
the next I was cross-eyed with my nose pressed
up against a donkey's rear
end. Not the nicest
thing I've smelt
today!

How in the
name of all the
gods did it happen?
It was spooky – as if
someone had thumped
into me from behind. It
nearly took all the breath out
of my body, but I must have had some breath left,
because I shouted, 'Yeeow!'

Or did I? Maybe the voice was just in my head. Anyway, it took me ages to get over it. For a while my hands wouldn't do what I wanted them to. It was as if I'd never brushed a donkey before. And when it came to putting on the halter! My little sister Sophronia could have done better than that, and she's pretty daft.

Whatever was the matter with me? I've worked with donkeys all my life. Now I was behaving as if I'd never been near one before, getting bitten, treading in donkey doo - it was almost as if I was someone else.

But I'm not someone else. I'm me, Nikoleon, and this is where I belong.

Tomorrow I have to help Father start the wheat harvest. He's been sharpening tools for days (while I see to all four donkeys totally on my own). Our land is quite rocky and hilly, so we can't plant much wheat; just enough for our own bread really, and a bit to swap with neighbours for other things we need. It won't take long to

harvest, and that worries Father. He says the farm
is getting poorer. That's because the stream that
feeds our land only has half the water in it that it
used to. If the ground's too dry, there's not

enough grass for the goats and sheep, and the soil itself blows away. What use is a farm without good soil?

No wonder Father gets a bit scratchy sometimes.

🐝 🐝 🐝

Typical! We worked from sunrise on the wheat, and just when it was time to stop for some food and a quick zizz in the olive grove, someone wants two donkeys! And of course she wants to hire me, as well.

It was Melissa, the bee woman, wanting to

deliver pots of honey to all her regular customers. I hate honey deliveries. OK, she supplies her own panniers to carry the pots in, but they're all sticky and oozy, and they attract everything that flies. I wouldn't touch her honey with a threshing shovel. I bet it's full of ants and drowned wasps.

Melissa keeps well back because, she says, she doesn't want to catch my fleas. Cheek! They're not my fleas. They're the donkeys' fleas. They just rest on me now and then. Silly woman – you soon get used to flea bites, but nothing would get me used to bee stings.

Father wouldn't let me take a third donkey to ride on. 'Give the others a rest,' he said. 'The walk will do you good.'

Huh. I know the donkeys need a rest day now and then to keep them healthy, but I need rest, too. Could there possibly be a worse job for me than donkey driver? There are plenty of other things I could do.

I get really fed up with walking. I walk

uphill, downhill, into the city, down to the harbour – anywhere people pay me to go. Well, they pay Father, not me, which makes it worse, because he never walks anywhere, not even  to the Assembly, which is no distance at all. When I'm old enough to go to the Assembly, I shall have the most handsome donkey in the world to ride on, so people will say, 'There's Niko – he's an important citizen! Let him speak first!'

When I got home, all I wanted to do was draw a bucket of cool water from the well and stick my feet into it. But first I had to wash down the donkey who'd carried the honey, and unstick his honey-gummed coat.

Now it's evening, and the sun's lost its heat. I've just played a game of draughts with Sophronia. She's a terrible cheat, but I always let her win. If I don't, she whines until I play again.

And again. She has to end up winning, or she won't go to bed happy.

✿ ✿ ✿

My brother Stephanos gave me a lesson when it was barely light this morning. We can only afford for one of us to go to school and he's older than me, so he goes. But Father's crafty. He makes my brother repeat his lessons to me. You'd think Stephanos wouldn't bother, but he's such a goody-goody – always does exactly as he's told. If Father told him to roll in the donkey-doo pile then jump off the nearest cliff, singing, 'I'm a pretty butterfly,' I reckon he would.

Steph got into trouble with his teacher yesterday, for untidy writing, so today he made me tidy up my letters. I had to smooth over my wax tablet three times before he was satisfied. It was really scruffy – I've never done it that badly before, not since I was little. It didn't even look like my writing. When I compared my first effort with my last, the first could almost have been someone else's.

I don't think I'll be doing many lessons for a while. Father keeps hinting that he's got a special job for me. I hope it's a sitting-down job. That'd be great. No more walking hour after hour, day after day. I hate walking. It's a complete waste of time.

Later

There's a white-bearded old man called Andreas who lives just inside the Athens city wall, not all that far from where we live. He sent a messenger to our farm today. Father is to go to Andreas's house, and he's all excited.

'Perhaps Andreas wants someone to work for him!' he said, as we picked almonds. 'They say he has a country estate, with a big farm. Perhaps he needs a new manager! Perhaps he'll employ me!'

Some hopes. Keep dreaming, Father! 'He has a secret hoard of treasure,' I said.

Father put his full basket down and pulled an empty one towards him. 'How do you know?'

'One of our slaves – Harmonia, I think – told me Andreas keeps a box under his bed, and only one of his slaves, called Hilarion, is ever allowed in that room.'

'Pah!' said Father. 'What can Harmonia know?'

'Whenever you send her to market,' I said, 'she talks to everyone she meets. She said the box is wrapped round and round with strips of leather. Andreas has melted wax over the leather knots and written his initial in the wax. That way, he'd know instantly if anyone had tampered with his box.'

'I suppose it could be true,' said Father, as we moved on to the next tree. 'He's not a poor man, by any means.'

I'll say. Andreas lends money to people. When they pay him back, they have to give him a bit extra. Quite a big bit extra, Stephanos reckoned, when he explained how money-lending works. It's a good business to be in. Andreas must be very rich.

'When you go there –' I began, but Father interrupted with: 'Just WHAT do you think you're doing?'

'What?' I said. Then I looked in my basket. 'Where are all the almonds I picked?'

Father pointed.

There was a hole in my basket, and I'd left a neat line of almonds running all the way back to the tree we'd just left.

'Daft boy,' muttered Father. 'Carry on picking, while I take my full baskets back. You can mend that basket before you eat.'

Typical. I always do far more work than anyone else.

I continued thinking about Andreas. Maybe he needs a trusty assistant to look after his riches. I can add (a little) and can count money and write numbers. At least I think so. I'm not sure after the weird way I messed up my letters this morning. Let's see . . .

Yes, back to normal. Thank the gods.

Now I'm all excited. Father told me that Andreas wants to meet me. Me! It's so he can see what I'm like, and if I'm trustworthy. At least, that's what Father says, and he insists that's all he knows. So it can't be an ordinary old donkey job. But what is it?

Maybe, after tomorrow, I'll never have to trudge along stony tracks with donkeys ever again. No more searching for water for them. No more humping heavy loads. No more scraping donkey doo into piles.

First Father sent me to the women's room. Mother and Grandmother were there, squabbling over the weaving loom. How they stand being cooped up all the time, I don't know, but there it is. Father hardly ever allows them to go out. I'd hate that.

Mother presented me with a length of cloth she'd just finished making. 'This will make a nice new tunic,' she said, holding it up against me. 'And don't ruin it,' she went on. 'It takes me long enough weaving blankets and clothes for this family as it is. I'm not doing double for you, just because you're careless.'

Careless! Me! She ought to spend an hour with four donkeys, then she'd see how easy it is to get your clothes chewed up and sodden with donkey dribble.

'Why have I got a new tunic?' I asked. I

haven't had one since I caught my foot in a donkey's halter and got dragged along the track. That was the day three members of the Athens city council called to see Father. The first thing they saw was my dusty bottom!

'It's important that you look smart when you go to see Andreas,' she replied. 'Look at what you're wearing now. It's so short you'd shock the donkeys if you bent down.'

Is it my fault I grow?

Grandmother helped me fasten my belt, like she's done since I was tiny. Then she licked her thumb and wiped a blob of porridge from my mouth. Her spit was all warm. Ugh.

'Andreas is very rich,' she whispered. 'He's got treasure. Everyone knows that. If he hires our donkeys, it could be the first of many times, so we have to do a good job . . .'

We!

'Your father wants to make sure Andreas always hires our donkeys in the future,' she twittered in my ear. 'Then who knows? Perhaps Andreas has an estate in the country, and perhaps he'll make your father his farm manager, and perhaps we'll all move to a big house and have more slaves and perhaps . . .'

Women! What do they know! She's as bad as Father, I thought, as she prattled on with her wild dreams.

'Take no notice,' Mother whispered in my other ear. 'Things like that don't happen to people like us. You just make sure you look respectable and don't let your family down. And,' she added, 'if the job's well-paid, there might be an obol or two in it for you.'

Oh great, I thought. An obol or two? Hardly the start of Nikoleon's Great Fortune.

I'm to ride our oldest donkey, Butter. She's called that, because she's as soft as butter, not because she butts people. Bolter's the donkey for that. Butts you and bolts.

Off I went to wash Butter down and clean her halter. It's a bit messy after I dropped it in the disgusting bit by the river where everyone takes their goats to drink.

Next day

Early this morning, wearing my brand new tunic, I kissed Butter on the nose (you wouldn't do that to any of the other donkeys) and hopped on her back. Off we trotted downhill until we joined the main road into Athens.

Normally I talk to anyone I meet, but today I was too excited to bother. Maybe there's a whole new life in front of me!

I reached Andreas's house, and knocked. The doorkeeper opened it.

'I've come to see Andreas,' I said, politely. 'I'm Nikoleon, son of Demoleon. I'm expected.'

'Please enter.'

'Where can I leave my donkey?' I asked.

'Bring it in,' was the reply.

'Eh?' Was he mad? A donkey, in a rich man's courtyard?

'Those are the master's orders,' said another voice – a low, slow one. I looked past the door-keeper. There was the droopiest, most miserable-looking slave I've ever seen.

'I am Hilarion,' said the miseryguts. Hilarion means cheerful. Someone got that wrong!

He led me and Butter into a large courtyard. Andreas's house certainly is grand. He must have a very full treasure box!

Andreas was sitting on a bench, enjoying the early sunshine. I thought how very old he looked, like a grandfather. Which, as it turned out, is exactly what he is!

A girl of about seven sat on the tiled floor beside him, fiddling with a clay doll. It had arms and legs fastened on with thin strips of leather, so she could move them.

The girl waggled the doll's arm at me. 'Zozo says hello,' she said. She had the sweetest face, pale golden-yellow hair, and I thought she looked like a little goddess.

'This is my granddaughter,' said the old man. He ruffled her hair. 'Run along now, Chrysanthe. I need to speak with Nikoleon. Go and play with Hilarion.'

I'd rather play with a sleepy spider. More fun.

Andreas asked me all about myself. Did I think I was trustworthy? Honest? Loyal? Stupid questions. I was hardly going to say no.

Then he called Chrysanthe. 'I must think,' he told me. 'Amuse my granddaughter for a while.'

That was easy. Being a little girl, she'd never been near a donkey before – she can't have been outside much. Thanking the gods that I'd brought Butter, not Nipper, I showed her how to feed a donkey without getting bitten, and I let her stroke Butter's warm sides.

'I like her smell,' said Chrysanthe.

'I rubbed her down with new-cut hay before I came,' I said. Don't suppose Chrysanthe sees

much grass, here in the city.

'May I ride her?' she asked.

'If your grandfather says so.'

Chrysanthe threw her arms round me. 'I like you, Nikoleon!' she said.

Aaah. She's so sweet.

But just then, Andreas appeared and sent her indoors. I had the creepy feeling he'd been watching me.

'Come back tomorrow, Nikoleon,' he said. 'I've something for you to do and, afterwards, I will tell you my plans.'

And now I'm so excited I can't sleep. Father went on all evening about how we should try to get Andreas to use us all the time for his business. 'With a big farm in the country,' he said, 'he must have to transport stuff back and forth. If Andreas uses our donkeys – and you, Niko,' he said, 'it could make a big difference to our family.'

Then he told me our farm isn't just poor – it's failing. I sort of knew, but my stomach felt full of rocks when I heard the words.

'The soil gets poorer every year,' Father said, as Mother and Grandmother brought in his bedtime wine. 'The donkey-hire business is the only way forward.'

'How much can you earn with four donkeys and a boy who hates walking?' asked Grandmother as she mixed water into his wine. Honestly! I don't know how she has the nerve to speak to him like that!

'More donkeys!' he said brightly. 'That's the answer! Each time we earn money, I'll put some aside towards another donkey. Soon our strings of donkeys will be carrying goods and people all across the land! We'll be rich!'

Mother pushed Grandmother out of the door before she could say any more. But as she crossed the courtyard, I distinctly heard, 'Tchah! He's a dreamer. Always has been. Always will be.'

But Father was staring into his wine. 'Mmm,' he murmured. 'We'll be rich . . .'

We!

Next day

I made sure to take Butter with me today. It was a good decision, as it turned out. Andreas asked me to take Chrysanthe out for a few hours and show her the city. He gave me money to buy her some food. She's lucky he's letting her out. The furthest my sister Sophronia's ever been is the market in our nearest village, which is pretty pathetic. There's only olives and grapes and oil and pomegranates and stuff there.

But the agora in Athens is something else!

Chrysanthe's a greedy little thing. As we went round the stalls she made me buy boiled shrimps, an apple, bread, some cheese, four figs and two pomegranates.

She's such a dainty creature. She didn't spit the pomegranate seeds out. She just poked them out of her mouth into her cupped hand. She spoiled it a bit by grabbing my hand and plopping all the sucked seeds into it for me to get rid of. But I didn't mind. She's sweet.

By the time I took Chrysanthe home, the sun looked ready to plummet down to earth. Hilarion offered Chrysanthe a meal, but she groaned, said she couldn't eat a thing and flopped down by the fountain, dabbling her toes in the cool water.

Andreas called me into the main room. When I saw who was there, my stomach felt heavy enough to plummet to the ground, just like the sun. Father! Oh, gods, I thought. What have I done!

Andreas asked how our day went. I told him it was lovely. He glanced out at Chrysanthe.

'She seems happy,' he said. 'Well done, boy. Now I'll tell you my plan. I want to see the Olympic games. I have discussed it with your father, and I am hiring you and your donkeys for the journey.'

I nearly passed out! Olympia is practically on the other side of Greece!

'Oh good.' My voice came out like an ancient frog's – weak and croaky.

'Are you not happy to do this?'

Father's eyes widened and his mouth went tight.

I thought quickly. I'm not happy, but I can imagine how unhappy Father would be if I said so. And that wouldn't be any fun – he's quick with a stick is my father.

Andreas frowned. 'Why do you hesitate?'

I thought even more quickly. 'I was just thinking it might be dangerous. Soldiers from city-states we're at war with . . . or even Spartans . . .' I've often had nightmares about Spartans, with their fighting women, and their tough children and their deadly fierceness.

Behind me Hilarion snorted.

Andreas was kinder. 'Haven't you heard of the Olympic truce?' he asked.

I shook my head.

'There's a period of time when peace is

declared, so all who wish to travel to the Olympic games may do so in safety. There's no danger. So, you will take on this task?'

I nodded. What else could I do?

'Then that's settled,' said Andreas. 'Now go and wash your feet in the fountain while I speak with your father.'

I looked down. My feet were black. And so were all the filthy footprints I'd left on Andreas's clean floor. I left, taking giant steps so as to leave as few extra prints as possible.

I sat down beneath the window and picked the muck out from between my toes. I could hear every word from inside, just as I'd hoped.

'Demoleon,' said Andreas, 'I have an estate in the country, and my farm manager is getting old and wishes to retire. I shall need a new one.'

My heart leapt.

'I've enjoyed meeting you to discuss my journey,' Andreas continued. 'I feel I can trust you. I wonder if you know of anyone you could recommend for the farm manager's job. Perhaps you'd think about it and let me know when I return from Olympia? Thank you, and good day.'

I shot across to the fountain and dunked my feet, just as Father came out into the courtyard, looking downcast.

'Come back tomorrow, Nikoleon,' called Andreas. 'I have more work for you while I prepare for my journey.'

Father was silent all the way home. I didn't say anything about the farm manager's job. He'd box my ears for letting them flap too much.

Now I'm in bed. My brother is jealous that I will see the games. Father has seen the Athens games but knows he'll probably never see the Olympics.

'Not unless you please Andreas,' he said. 'Then who knows what might happen? Just think of the future.'

'What is the future?' I asked.

He sighed. 'Donkeys, son. I'm afraid it's donkeys. Only donkeys.'

I never think of the future. I just think of today. But tonight I'm thinking of tomorrow. Will I be taking Chrysanthe out again?

Next day

Ooh, today was a bit different! Andreas suggested I show Chrysanthe the Parthenon, so we headed up to the Acropolis.

'Let's go to the agora,' said Chrysanthe, leaning forward to pat Butter's stubby mane. 'I can see the Acropolis from my bedroom window any time I like.'

'Ah, but you haven't seen what's up there,' I said.

38

She stuck out her bottom lip. 'I want to go to the agora.'

'Well, you can't,' I said.

She kicked Butter!

I was livid! 'You're lucky you're not on Bolter,' I said. 'You'd be halfway to the coast by now. If you managed to stay on.'

Didn't I see a different side of her then!

'I would have stayed on,' she said, tossing her head. 'Riding's easy.'

Hah! After two days she thinks she's an expert! She wants to be on Digfoot when he decides he's not going any further. He stops, but you don't!

'Tell you what,' I said. 'We'll do what your grandfather says and go to the Acropolis. If you behave nicely, I'll show you the theatre . . .'

That cheered her up, but she ignored me until we got to the top of the Acropolis. When she saw the statue of Athena, her chin nearly hit Butter's back.

'I never dreamed it would be this big,' she said.

On the way back downhill, Chrysanthe wanted to speed up.

'If you do, Butter will fall and break her leg, then your grandfather won't be able to go to the Olympics,' I said.

'Don't care,' she said, and kicked Butter's sides.

'Stop!' I yelled, as my donkey trotted

unsteadily down the steep hill, her hooves skittering on loose stones. I slowed her down, and turned to tell Chrysanthe off.

Her face! She'd pinched her lips together. They looked like a grape that's been in the sun for months – all creased and shrunken. Her eyes were narrow slits. Where was the little golden-haired angel?

'Don't speak to me like that,' she snapped, 'or I'll tell Grandfather!'

I was furious. 'And don't you speak to me like that,' I warned her, 'or I'll tell your grandfather what a rude, bad-tempered, bossy little brat you are. And before you say any more, I'm not a slave, whatever you think.'

She sniffed. 'You're a donkey boy. And you've got fleas. You're a fleabag!' she shouted, right in my face.

Little beast. How could I have ever thought her sweet?

After that outburst, I refused to take her to the theatre. She went into a real sulk and, to make matters worse, when we got back, Hilarion said I'm to take her out again tomorrow. I had something on my mind, so I never said anything about how she behaved today. Instead I asked to see Andreas.

He shrugged and plodded away. 'Don't expect so . . .'

He was still muttering when he plodded back. 'Go in.'

Andreas was lying on a couch. He looked tired.

'Nikoleon,' he said, 'my granddaughter enjoys being with you. Do you enjoy being with her?'

'I do,' I lied.

'Good. What did you wish to say to me?'

Wondering if two lies would be too much for

the gods, I told him I couldn't help overhearing about his farm manager retiring. I asked if he'd be kind enough to consider my father for the job. 'He's a good farmer,' I said. 'He knows all about the land, and animals, and he'd work so hard for you, and . . . and . . .' I saw Hilarion's grey shadow slide past the doorway. 'And he's very cheerful and always looks on the bright side of things.'

Andreas seemed taken aback. 'But you have a farm already, and your donkey business, too.'

'The farm's not thriving,' I said, and I told him about the lack of water, and the soil drying out, and how the land's getting poorer, and everything. 'Father thinks our future has to lie with the donkeys.'

I stopped. I suddenly couldn't bear to think of my future, trailing donkeys back and forth until I'm an old man. I want a treasure box, too – even just a little one.

'Please don't tell him I asked,' I said. 'He'd be embarrassed.' And I'd be for it, I thought.

'I see,' said Andreas. 'Well, Nikoleon, I like your father. He seems a good, honest man, and I know he is well thought of. That's why I went to him to hire donkeys for my journey.'

He looked down and was quiet for so long I thought he'd dropped off. Then he lifted his head so suddenly that I jumped.

'Let's complete our journey together, then I'll give you my decision. If I'm pleased with you, I'm sure I'll be pleased with the father who brought you up.'

I caught my breath.

'However,' he went on, 'I have asked other

44

people to look for a new farm manager for me, so, in the meantime, it would be best if you said nothing to your father. It would be cruel to get his hopes up in vain. Can you manage that?'

'Oh yes. Thank you.'

The sooner we get off to the Olympics, then, the better. I never thought I'd think that, but I do.

As I rode home, it dawned on me that if I do a good job for Andreas, it will mean Father becomes his farm manager. And Grandmother's mutterings might mean something after all. Perhaps we could all move into a big house . . . perhaps we could have more slaves and perhaps . . .

Anything is possible!

Next day

Freedom! Almost. Andreas's messenger came to say that I'm to take the little yellow-haired viper out tomorrow instead of today.

'Chrysanthe is a little sore where she sits

45

down,' said Father with a grin. 'Too much riding all at once!'

Why doesn't she give it up altogether, I wondered – give us all a bit of Olympic peace.

'You'll need all four donkeys for your journey,' said Father. 'One for Andreas, two for baggage, food and water, and one for you. You wouldn't want to walk all that way!'

I laughed. Imagine walking to Olympia!

Next day

My orders, from Andreas, were to take the little yellow viper to the theatre (we weren't to see a play, because it was unsuitable) and I could take her to see anything else she fancied.

That's every market stall that sells food, then, I thought.

'Tell one of the theatre attendants that I have asked you to show my granddaughter round,' said Andreas. 'He will let you.'

I doubted that! All the attendants I've heard about have been pretty handy with their sticks. They're only supposed to use them if there's serious trouble in the audience, but Father says power goes to their heads.

I was wrong! When I mentioned Andreas's name, not one, but two attendants, showed us round. They even found a honey cake from the actors' dressing room for Chrysanthe. Nice to see a smile back on her snappy little face. How I ever imagined her to be like a goddess, I can't imagine.

They left us to have a look through the costumes, and I found a box of masks. Chrysanthe put on one, and it looked like a woman, crying. It was huge. No wonder the audience can see how the actors are feeling from anywhere in the theatre. I put on a scary one, and turned and went, 'Boo!'

The effect was staggering! Did she scream! You'd have thought a pack of wolves were after her. Men ran from all sides to see who was being murdered. A young one, dressed in a woman's chiton, calmed her and fetched her a cool drink. The others scolded me for being unkind. What did I think I was doing, frightening a delicate little creature like this? I should be whipped!

As we left, Chrysanthe looked at me slyly, and grinned. The little viper hadn't been scared at all. She just screamed so she could get me into trouble.

We're off the day after tomorrow, and I'll be

glad to see the back of her. Thank goodness I've finished with Chrysanthe.

🦐 🦐 🦐

Today Mother baked all day. I took my sandals to be repaired, then sneaked the donkeys on to some good pasture on someone's else's good grass, lower down the valley.

When we got back, I went to put the donkeys away for the night, and stopped at the door in surprise. I'd left a nice clean, empty stable, and what did I find? Piles of fresh donkey doo everywhere and, in the corner, a new donkey.

Father called to me, 'What do you think? Fine animal, isn't she?'

'Whose is she?' I asked.

'Ours.'

'Ours! But we can't afford another donkey,' I said without thinking.

Stephanos came past on his way back from school. 'Don't speak to Father like that,' he said. 'He knows what he's doing. Father has a plan for the future, and this must be part of it.'

Hah! Plan! More like a dream.

'But why? Why buy another donkey?' I asked.

'It's an investment,' said Father. 'As Stephanos says, it's part of my plan for the future. Demoleon's Donkeys! Ours will be the sturdiest and fastest donkeys in the land. Everybody will want to hire them.'

Father's spent all that money, and I'm sure he can't afford it. Maybe he's even borrowed it. How will he pay it back? Not till we get paid for the Olympic trip, that's certain.

'But just suppose,' I began, 'just suppose

Andreas has got a farm, and just suppose he wants a manager –'

'He *has* got a farm,' Father said, 'and he *does* want a manager.'

'Well, then –'

'If he wanted me, he would have asked me, wouldn't he?' Father snapped. 'And he hasn't.'

'Perhaps if he knew our farm was failing . . .'

Father whirled round. 'Shut up! Why do you think I want to build up the donkey business? I want people to think, "Demoleon's doing well. He's using his land just to grow food for the family, and he's building up a large donkey business." I don't want them to know our farm's failing. I've got my pride!'

Oops. I hope Andreas never lets on that I said anything.

'Sorry, Niko.' Father ruffled my hair. 'Go and settle the donkeys for the night – Nipper looks as if he wants to pick a fight with someone – then food and an early night. Tomorrow you're off to Olympia. Lucky boy!'

Just as I was going to bed Father said, 'Take the new donkey on your journey.'

'I will,' I said. 'It'll mean I can rest one donkey every day in turn.'

He gazed at the moon – dreaming, I suppose. 'You can't,' he said. 'The extra donkey's for Andreas's slave. It was stupid of me to imagine a man like Andreas would travel without a slave! Night, Niko.'

A slave. Oh, please, Hermes, god of travellers . . . don't let it be Hilarion.

I had all five donkeys ready before dawn – Butter, Nipper and Digfoot for riding, the others for baggage. Both carried panniers, ready to be filled. I soon named the new donkey – Twitchy. Every time I touched her, her ears twitched, her tail flicked, her hooves pattered and her sides shivered.

Everyone got up to say goodbye. Father thumped my back and said, 'See you when you get home.' Steph gripped my arms, looked into my eyes, and said, 'See you do well, Nikoleon.'

Pompous pig.

Sophronia squeezed me. 'I'll miss you. Will you bring me back a present?' she asked.

Grandmother said, 'He'll bring himself back. That's all we ask of him and the gods.' She kissed me on both cheeks, and on my forehead. 'Wherever you sleep, Nikoleon,' she said, 'look up at the stars, and know that we're looking at those same stars and thinking of you.'

That made my eyes go teary. But then she licked her thumb . . .

Mother made me promise to wash my clothes and clean my ears. Father whispered, 'Do the best job you can.' I thought he meant with my ears for a moment, but then he continued, 'If Andreas is pleased, he'll tell his rich friends about our donkey service. It could mean a brighter future for us.'

Father doesn't know quite how important it is that Andreas is pleased. If he's not, he'll never make Father his manager. Oh, just imagine! We could sell our land, and live and work on Andreas's farm, making wine and olive oil and growing things, and I'd have slaves to clear up all the donkey doo . . .

Now I'm dreaming!

As I turned to leave, I had an awful thought. 'But I don't know the way!'

Father laughed. 'Hundreds of people will be making their way to Olympia. Tell Digfoot to follow them!'

That made everyone smile, which was a good time to go. I waved until my donkey train had rounded a rocky outcrop and I could no longer see home.

I was on my way! The longest journey of my life!

Andreas's courtyard was full of slaves and bags. They loaded Bolter and Twitchy, who were carrying baggage, and I made sure they did it properly, so the weight was balanced.

'One more thing,' said Hilarion, handing me a box made of pale wood and tied with leather thongs. It was sealed with a blob of beeswax, into which was carved a letter A.

The treasure box!

'Take great care of this,' said Hilarion. 'Fasten it tightly. Don't let it fall or you'll be for it.'

'What is it?' I asked innocently.

'The master's keepsake box,' said Hilarion. 'It's one of his most important possessions, and he

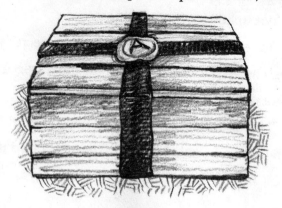

never travels without it. Nothing to do with you.'

More's the pity. I tied the box on to Twitchy. She shivered and shuddered, but there was no chink or rattle from the box. Everything inside must be wrapped in cloth.

I'd chosen Butter for Andreas, but he ignored her and mounted Digfoot.

'This one's stubborn,' I said. 'If Digfoot wants to stop, he digs his feet in, and nobody goes anywhere until he's ready. And if you're going fast when he stops –'

'Digfoot and I will get on well,' said Andreas. 'If you lead, I'm sure he will follow you.'

OK, I thought. I'll ride Butter and rope Digfoot to her.

I'd saved Nipper for Hilarion. Secretly I hoped he'd take a chunk out of the old miseryguts before we started. But where had he got to?

'Hello, Niko!' called Chrysanthe. I couldn't see her at first – only Hilarion. Then I realised that the fat bundle he was carrying was Chrysanthe, all muffled up against the early morning chill. He put her down, and she waddled over to Butter.

'Well?' she said. 'Help me up, Niko.'

I must have had a strange expression on my face, because Andreas burst out laughing.

'Is Chrysanthe coming?' I asked in disbelief.

'Most certainly,' Andreas said firmly. 'She is the only member of my family left. I want her with me. I can't leave her behind with slaves. I must look after her.'

I remembered the tale I'd heard of how Andreas's son and his whole family were shipwrecked. The only one saved was his six-month-old granddaughter. A sailor had struggled ashore with her. The story went that the sailor was rewarded so well he's now got his own fleet of ships.

Andreas smiled. 'Didn't you wonder why I asked you to spend time with Chrysanthe? She had to learn to ride, and to get used to you and the donkeys before we undertake our journey.'

No, I didn't wonder. I'm stupid. I just thought he wanted me to see she had a good time before he went away.

'I want you to be her friend,' Andreas continued. 'She needs young company.'

OK, if he wants to take Chrysanthe – a girl – that's fine with me, I thought. I kept quiet and helped her on to Butter.

Hilarion sat slumped on Nipper, who turned his head and eyed the slave's long legs. I know my donkey well, and it seemed to me he fancied taking a little nip out of Hilarion. That cheered me up.

'Right,' I said. 'Let's go.'

It was at that moment it dawned on me. The bags were packed, everyone was mounted, but –

I didn't have a donkey.

'I – I've got to walk?' I spluttered.

Nobody was listening. All Andreas's slaves were waving and shouting goodbye. I took Butter's halter, and led the donkey train out through the gate – the first steps on our journey to Olympia.

Oh joy! Blessings on Poseidon, god of the sea. We're on a ship!

To be exact, we're on two ships. Andreas, Chrysanthe and Hilarion are on one, and I'm on the other, with the donkeys. There was I, thinking we'd have to walk all the way to Olympia! Instead, we've walked (well, I have) down to the port of Piraeus.

When we arrived, a sailor leapt from the deck and ran to hug first Chrysanthe, who looked slightly shocked, and then Andreas. It turns out that he's the one who saved Chrysanthe's life when she was a baby, and we're on two of his ships. I expect we'll sail along the coast as far as possible, then go overland for the last bit.

 Oh woe! Poseidon, protector of sailors, hear my prayer and end my misery.

The ships heave from side to side, and the front goes up and then it plunges down, up and down . . .

I haven't stopped throwing up since we left the harbour. There's donkey doo everywhere, and the sailors kept bellowing at me to clear it up.

Now the sea's rougher than ever. The sailors have stopped bawling at me. They're too worried about keeping us afloat.

I'm glad my mother and grandmother don't know the danger I am in.

I'm still being sick.

A sailor told me that as soon as the sea calms, we're putting into the nearest harbour. Andreas's orders. Sometimes I catch sight of him on the ship ahead, roped to the mast so he doesn't get washed overboard. He always clutches Chrysanthe in his arms. He must be terrified he'll lose her, as he lost the rest of his family.

This morning, instead of trying to eat my breakfast, I threw it into the sea as a sacrifice to Poseidon. To be honest, if I'd eaten it, it would have ended up over the side anyway, but Poseidon doesn't know that. I don't think so, anyway.

Later

My sacrifice worked. Poseidon calmed the wind, and smoothed the sea. While we made for shore, I was kept busy washing down the deck and getting the donkeys ready.

Three days we've been travelling now. At first the going was easy, through farmland. Then we began to climb a narrow mountain track. The donkeys skitter and slip. So do I! Chrysanthe keeps grumbling about her rear end. I've padded her donkey's back as much as possible. She has all my clothes to sit on, yet still she moans. Hilarion is fuming, because Andreas has ordered him to take turns with me, so while one rides, the other walks. Andreas is a fair man.

At night we stop. Hilarion builds a fire and gets our food ready, Andreas rests with his treasure box beside him, I see to the donkeys, and Chrysanthe gets bored. I feel a bit sorry for her. All she has is her doll, Zozo, some knucklebones and some dice. Of course, no one wants to play

with her until the work's done. I usually take the donkeys a distance away to graze, so I can get some peace. This evening, I led them back and as I neared our camp, I heard Chrysanthe.

'Hilarion, will you please have fun.'

'I am having fun,' he lied.

'Then why aren't you smiling?' she demanded.

'I am,' he muttered. 'I'm smiling inside.'

The moment she saw me, she made me play knucklebones with her. And, I soon found out, she likes to win. She's a worse cheat than my sister. But I have to be nice to her. Andreas made it clear that part of my job is to keep her happy, and if that keeps him happy, then keep her happy I will. Even if it drives me crazy.

Hilarion is a selfish pig. He lies about how long he's been riding, so I walk the most. Andreas ignores our arguing. Chrysanthe tells us to shut up. She makes me so angry, talking to me as if I was a slave! Who does she think she is? All the money they have doesn't make her any better than me.

My legs are so tired.

Today I had a proper ride! We'd just cleared camp when we heard shouting and the rumble of wheels. Andreas made us stand back in the trees until we saw who it was. He says you can't be too careful, in spite of the Olympic truce. I took the donkey carrying the treasure box behind some thick undergrowth.

A man riding a mule appeared, followed by a cart and, behind that, a chain of naked men. I say a chain, because they were linked together by a rope tied to the cart. The rope was threaded

through collars round their necks. Behind came two more men on mules, then another small cart.

Andreas moved forward, lifting a hand. The men on mules raised a hand in return. Their leader signalled them to stop, then dismounted and stretched himself. The men in the chain collapsed to the ground and sat, silent.

'We need water,' said the lead man, once he and Andreas had greeted each other and grumbled about the state of the track.

'There's a river down in the valley,' I called. 'I can see water sparkling in the sun.'

'Thanks, boy,' said the man.

Andreas took a goat skin from Bolter's pannier. 'We can offer you a little water now,' he said, 'but we don't have much.'

The man dismounted. 'I'm grateful,' he said. 'I'll share the skin amongst my men.'

He drank, then passed the skin to the cart drivers and mule riders. When they'd drunk, there was a little left. I expected him to give it to the roped men, but he didn't. Instead, he tipped it over his head and face.

'That feels good!' he said, handing the skin back. 'I hope you find kindness from strangers on the road, as we have.'

I took another skin and was going to offer it to the men in the rope chain, but Andreas stepped on my foot. I yelped and looked up at him. His expression said, 'Shut up, Niko.' So I did. But I think it unkind not to share the water equally.

The mule train left. I put Chrysanthe on Butter, and tied Bolter and Nipper, who were carrying packs for the day, behind. Andreas and Hilarion followed.

Chrysanthe fidgeted once she was on Butter's back. 'Grandfather! I want to go home!'

'We're over halfway, child,' he said. 'It's a shorter journey to Olympia than it is to home.'

'Then can't Niko make me more comfortable?'

I took a deep breath. 'Chrysanthe, if you sit

on anything more, you'll be so high up you'll get your head knocked off as we pass under the next tree.' Which wouldn't be a bad idea, I thought.

Andreas, as usual, just gazed around. Hilarion sat on his donkey and drooped. His arms drooped, his body drooped, his mouth drooped, his eyes drooped – even his hair drooped.

Eventually, we caught up with the mule train going up a steep slope. The driver turned, saw me leading Butter and said, 'Haven't you got a ride, boy? Hop on the cart. We go at walking pace because of these lazy fellows.' He meant the prisoners, and he didn't actually say 'fellows'. I won't repeat the word he used.

I jumped on the back of the cart and sat facing Chrysanthe, holding her lead rope. She stuck her tongue out, and called, 'Grandfather, is Niko allowed to do that? Shouldn't he walk beside me?'

Andreas said, 'It's good that Niko can rest his feet. And you, granddaughter, are a good enough rider not to need him beside you all the time.'

Didn't she smirk! It's only Butter's gentle nature that makes her a good rider. I'd like to put her on Bolter and give him a whack. That'd show whether she was good or not!

The cart driver tossed me a couple of ripe figs. I slurped as much as I could as I ate the first one. Chrysanthe licked her lips.

I immediately wolfed the second one. She did her shrivelled-grape-lips look again.

The driver turned sideways so he could talk to me. 'Where are you bound for?'

'The Olympic games,' I said. 'And you?'

'To the silver mines. This lot,' he said, pointing his whip at the roped men, 'are going to have a new career. Miners!'

'Sounds exciting,' I said. 'Silver's very valuable. They'll soon be rich. I'd like to be a miner.'

The man laughed. 'Only the mine owners are rich! These are slaves, and I'd bet every drachma I own they'll all be dead within two years. It's a dangerous life – bad air underground, and rock falls every so often.'

I thought of our own slaves, and how they have good food and fresh air and water when they want it. Then I looked at the poor souls ahead, walking in misery to their deaths. I turned away from the driver.

Chrysanthe glared at me. 'I wish you were a

silver miner.'

She can be quite nasty when she doesn't get what she wants. I'd better tread carefully – I've a feeling it wouldn't be a good idea to upset her.

Just before midday, the mining people branched on to a different track, so I had to walk again. The path was quite smooth and my legs were fresh, so I didn't mind too much.

We headed down a steep slope into a valley, and stopped by a tumbling stream to rest while the sun was at its highest. Andreas settled beneath some leafy flowering trees and I took the donkeys to drink.

When I'd finished, Hilarion asked me to go and hunt for fruit.

'I'll come,' said Chrysanthe.

'You won't,' I said.

'I will!' Her lips shrivelled.

'You won't,' said Hilarion, agreeing with me for once. 'Suppose a bear attacked you. This puny boy couldn't save you. Stay with me.'

I laughed to myself. Some choice. Bitten to death or bored to death!

Chrysanthe stamped. 'I want to go!'

'This isn't bear country,' said Andreas. 'No animals will be prowling about in this heat. Just don't wander far. And, Niko – mind you look after my precious girl.'

Why does he always give in to her?

I stalked off, Chrysanthe behind me, but once we were out of Hilarion's sight, I broke off a dead branch – just in case anything fierce was lurking nearby.

We found figs, and almonds, and some not

very ripe pears.

'I'm going down to paddle,' said Chrysanthe.

'No,' I said. 'You heard your grandfather. Don't wander off. If you do, I'll call him.'

I turned my back on her furious face and tried a hard green pear to see if it was edible.

I'd barely sunk my teeth into it when there was a blood-curdling scream behind me. I turned, my heart pounding, to see

Chrysanthe, mouth wide open, roaring as if an eagle had her in its talons.

Hilarion crashed down the hill, with

Andreas, white-faced, stumbling after him.

'A wolf!' she cried. 'Grandfather, it was a wolf! And Niko left me to be eaten!'

'What? What?'

'The wolf ran off when I screamed,' she sobbed. I say 'sobbed', but there were no tears to be seen.

Andreas hugged Chrysanthe and helped her back uphill as she spouted her lies. I don't believe there was a wolf. If there was, wouldn't I have heard it?

Hilarion grabbed my tunic and my branch, and started to lay about me.

'Where's the wolf?' I spluttered, as I tried to dodge the blows. 'If there was one, where is it?'

'It ran, thanks be to great Hera, when it heard the child's terrified screams,' he growled. 'Take that!'

'Ow!'

'And that!'

'Ow!'

73

Hilarion beat me! A slave beat me! And I daren't complain, because Andreas is still so angry.

No one spoke to me for the rest of the day. I had to walk, of course. I really hate Hilarion. And Chrysanthe. Even Andreas. Nobody bothered to get my side of the story. At times like this, I think of my family. Even Stephanos would believe I'm innocent, and that's saying something.

Life isn't fair.

After hours of trudging, the sun was well down, when Andreas called to Chrysanthe, who was riding behind me, 'Ask Niko to stop, child. We'll camp here.'

'Yes, Grandfather,' she said sweetly, then, to me, 'Hoy! Fleabag! Stop!'

If looks could kill, she'd have been splattered on the track in a million slimy pieces.

Two days I've walked, with not a hint of being offered a ride on one of my own donkeys. The track's busy now. We're often passed by people walking to the Olympics. Sometimes we pass others. Everyone goes at their own pace, and there's plenty of friendly chat. Oh, you get the odd bad-tempered person, but he's usually riding. You can tell if someone's in a bad mood as you come up behind them, because their legs flap like bats' wings as they kick their mules. The walkers are more cheerful.

Some evenings, we allow a traveller to join us for a meal, but he's never allowed to sleep near us. Every night, Hilarion has to dig a shallow hole and put the treasure box in it. Then he throws a blanket over it and sleeps with his head on it. Every night, he grumbles himself to sleep because the box is so hard. Every night, Andreas moves further away to escape all that moaning.

This afternoon, after a midday meal of beans, cheese and fresh bread, which we bought from a farm, we snoozed in the shade of some short, thick trees, growing against the cliff-like mountainside. Afterwards, Andreas relented and let me ride. Hilarion was furious. I gave him the two pack donkeys to lead, mounted Nipper and went to the front of our little train. Anything rather than look at his head drooping between his shoulders.

We reached a level stretch of ground, littered with sharp stones, and Hilarion never stopped grumbling. Chrysanthe, fed up with him, kicked her donkey so it came alongside mine. I ignored her. I hate her. She amuses herself by getting me into trouble, just because I won't let her have her own way. She knows how important it is for me to please Andreas – I swear she does.

Even Andreas got fed up with Hilarion's whingeing.

'You've only walked a short way, man,' he said. 'Keep going and your feet will toughen.' He moved behind Chrysanthe, leaving Hilarion at the back.

I smiled to myself. Not for long, though. Chrysanthe fidgeted and bounced which made Butter sidestep every now and then. Nipper didn't like that.

'Drop back, Chrysanthe,' I said.

'No.'

'Then sit still. You're upsetting the donkeys,' I warned, urging Nipper to move ahead.

'I'm going in front,' she said, and she kicked, hard. Butter brayed and my donkey lived up to his name and nipped her. Butter danced sideways and Chrysanthe plopped to the ground.

It was no distance to fall, but by the din she made, you'd think she'd been hurled down a mountain. Everybody went to help her up.

'It's that horrible boy,' she said. 'He wouldn't let me go in front. He made his donkey bite Butter.' She glared at me. 'Fleabag!'

Oh no! I eyed Hilarion, who looked smug. He was clearly thinking, 'That's Nikoleon's ride finished – Andreas will make him walk now.'

But Andreas, though he didn't call Chrysanthe a liar or anything, insisted I'd done nothing wrong. 'Let's mount our donkeys and keep moving,' he said.

I stayed still.

'You too, Nikoleon,' he said.

I smiled at Hilarion. His face!

🐜 🐜 🐜

That droopy miserable slave is such a liar. We'd hardly got going after the nipping incident, when he cried out and collapsed on the track.

'Help him, Niko!' said Andreas.

I jumped down, handed Nipper's rein to Chrysanthe and said, 'Stay still and hold that tight.'

Hilarion was writhing on the ground, clutching his ankle. He pointed to a large stone. 'I trod on that! My ankle's broken.'

Andreas reached us and felt the ankle. 'No bones broken, Hilarion – merely a bad sprain. But you cannot walk. Nikoleon,' he said. 'Fetch your donkey. I'm afraid your ride is over.'

I was so fed up that, until I reached Chrysanthe, I didn't notice that she and Butter stood alone. 'Where's Nipper?' I asked.

'I don't know,' she said. 'He's your donkey.'

'Andreas!' I called. 'I must find Nipper! Chrysanthe let him go!'

Instead of telling Chrysanthe what a stupid little brat she is, he told me to come and help Hilarion into the shade. Personally, I'd have left him out to cook. My donkey's more important. Suppose someone found him and stole him?

I pulled Hilarion, not too gently, under a fig tree, and sat him on some over-ripe, slightly rotten fallen figs. Nice!

I picked some juicy grasses and sprinkled them with cool water, then went to look for my donkey. Chrysanthe followed. I hope she felt guilty.

I found Nipper without too much trouble. Chrysanthe watched me lure him close and let him eat some of the moist grass, so I could grab his halter. Keeping the rest of the grass just in front of his nose, I led him back to the others.

Chrysanthe watched the whole time.

'You know how to catch a donkey now,' I said. 'If you ever lose yours, you can fetch it yourself. Or walk.'

And now I walk. All the way.

Last night Andreas exploded. He'd had enough of Hilarion's night noises. 'Nikoleon, I'm trusting you with my keepsake box now,' he said. 'Guard it well.'

It was an honour to be trusted, but I'm annoyed that Hilarion's got rid of the job of guarding it. He and Chrysanthe certainly know how to get their own way.

🐜 🐜 🐜

Andreas is getting tired. We don't camp out now if we don't have to. We try to find some sort of lodging each night. I always end up sleeping with the donkeys, but one night we stayed at a big house with proper stabling. The women of the house clucked over Chrysanthe like old hens, and took her to their rooms to sleep. My bed was a straw-stuffed mattress in the servants' quarters. It was so comfortable! I couldn't sleep on top of the treasure box, so I tied it to me and cuddled it all night. It only had eight corners when I went to bed, but by the time I got up, it felt as if it had a hundred!

When we met next morning, Chrysanthe was all clean and shiny and fresh. She even seemed sweeter-natured for a while, until she got back on Butter. She finds riding very uncomfortable. Good.

The road – it's more than a track now – gets busier by the day. People are travelling from all over, as if the whole world wants to see the Olympic games! No foreigners are allowed, though – but Greeks who live in other lands can come.

Chrysanthe looked for athletes, but Andreas said we wouldn't see any. 'They all go to a village called Elis, to train, a month before the games. They've trained for ten months before that – in fact they must swear to that at the start of the games. At Elis they're watched carefully. Only those of a good enough standard may enter.'

Andreas knows a lot about the Olympics. Perhaps he's been before.

Now the road's so busy, local people stand at

the side and sell food and drink. One thing I'll say about Andreas – he's not mean. And having a pig like Chrysanthe with us means we get food regularly. She can't pass a woman with a tray of fresh bread or cakes, or a man with a basket of cooked fish, without stopping. Great!

🐛 🐛 🐛

Last night we stayed in a hut belonging to a potter. I watched him work. It's much better stuff than our village potter makes – his pots are plain clay. This man paints pots with a mixture of clay and water, called slip, and at last I know how the pictures on posh pots and bowls are coloured. When the potter fires them in his kiln, the painted bit turns black and the bare clay bit turns red. He let me have a go at painting a vase. I did a picture of our donkey train all the way round it.

Chrysanthe said my pot was only fit to pee in. Good idea – I could keep it by my bed and not have to go out at night. Pity there's no time for it to be fired.

🐙 🐙 🐙

Three more days have passed, and we're nearly at Olympia! The road's crowded at times, and everybody's in a good mood. We even have music to help us along!

I'm tired, though, and my donkeys will welcome a rest. But at least I'll be able to tell my family I walked practically all the way to Olympia.

OH NOOOOOOO!

I'm so dense. It's just dawned on me. I'll probably have to walk all the way back, too!

🐙 🐙 🐙

We're here! At Olympia! Thousands of people are camping around the sports ground. I've never seen so many men in one place before! Lots have been here for days already. More are arriving all the time. I've even seen people carrying boats! They've come by sea, and finished their journey by river. I only wish my mother and father could see through my eyes at this moment!

In the distance I can see the gymnasium where the athletes practise, and two temples, and lots of other buildings.

Overlooking it all is a hill, called the Hill of Kronos, where Zeus had a fight with his father. Imagine, me being so close to where the great god Zeus walked. Gives me shivers!

When I say we're at Olympia, we're almost there. Andreas called a halt just before we reached the vast camping site. 'We will stay beyond that grove,' he said, pointing to a group of ancient, gnarled trees.

Chrysanthe scowled. 'I want to go there,' she said, pointing to the crowds. She turned huge

eyes on her grandfather. 'Pleeeease?'

'No, Chrysanthe,' he said.

Oooh! Back came the scowl!

'Sport is a man's world,' Andreas explained. 'The athletes don't wear clothes, and men can be rough – sometimes their words aren't fit for a girl's pretty little ears.'

She turned her back on him! He should have boxed her pretty little ears.

I wove a path through the twisted trees, and came out on to a flat stretch of short, coarse grass. The donkeys immediately put their heads down and ripped at it. We unloaded everything and, while Hilarion crawled round unpacking (I predict that his ankle will heal miraculously now we're here) I walked further on to look for water.

The grass-covered ground sloped, gently at first, then steeply, down to a sheer drop. To one side there was an easy zigzag path to a river, probably trodden down by goats. At least I hope so. It could have been trodden by bears. Or wolves. It wasn't a big enough drop to call a cliff, but I made sure everyone knew it was there. I didn't want Andreas wandering off in the night for a pee, and falling over.

'We won't go that way,' Andreas reassured me. 'Nikoleon, I'll be walking to the games each day. Hilarion will accompany me when his ankle is better –'

Wow! That's the first time Hilarion's ever shown anything like a cheerful expression. He looked quite peculiar.

'Until then, he'll guard our camp,' Andreas continued, 'and my keepsake box. You and Chrysanthe may amuse yourselves, but, Nikoleon, you will guard her at all times. Understand? She's never to be out of your sight, except when she needs to relieve herself.'

'Relieve herself?' I said.

He rolled his eyes.

'Oh! Sorry!' I realised what he meant. Of course I'd turn my back when she did anything private. 'I'll watch her, don't worry.'

Great. Stuck with the yellow-haired viper all day.

🐜 🐜 🐜

As I predicted, there's been a little miracle. Hilarion woke this morning, cured.

'Look, Master!' he cried. 'I can walk!'

Andreas wasn't surprised. Perhaps he knows his slave is a liar.

'Get everything organised today for our comfort,' he told Hilarion, 'arrange for some fresh food, then tomorrow you may accompany me to the first day of the games.' He turned to me. 'While Hilarion begins his tasks, Nikoleon, you and Chrysanthe and I will take a walk.'

Hilarion gave me the filthiest glare.

Andreas took us through the bustling camping site, showing Chrysanthe all the entertainments. I liked the jugglers best. One was letting the spectators have a go, and I'd have like to, but Chrysanthe couldn't settle in one place for more than a moment. She'd hear a tambourine and would dart off looking for it, or she'd catch sight of an acrobat, or she'd smell food. 'Come and see!' she'd cry, tugging Andreas's hand. Off we'd all trot, doing what she wanted and watching her eat everything she could get her hands on.

I had an idea. If Chrysanthe wanted to watch the Olympic games, maybe Andreas would let us go with him. We could take turns with Hilarion. As we wandered past a noisy group, all drinking wine and laughing and joking, I whispered to her, 'Chrysanthe, the games go on for five days. They must be really exciting. Wouldn't you like to see them?'

She shrugged. 'Maybe.'

'Why don't you ask your grandfather?' I suggested, knowing he'd say yes if she asked.

'I might.' She skipped up to yet another food seller, looking appealingly at Andreas.

But she didn't ask him.

Andreas stopped to rest under a tree overlooking the games ground. I'd expected there to be just a running track and a hippodrome for the horse races, but it was like a large village. Andreas pointed out the Temple of Zeus. 'Inside,' he said, 'is a great wonder – a gold statue of Zeus.'

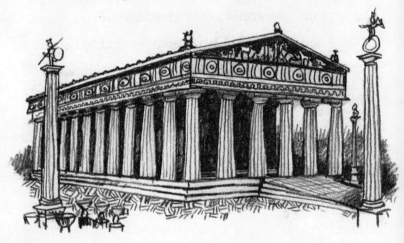

'What's so marvellous about that?' Chrysanthe said.

'It is as tall as eight men standing one on top of the other!' said Andreas.

That is a statue indeed! I should love to see it.

He pointed off to the left. 'See that square building? That's for visitors to stay in.'

'Can't we stay there?' Chrysanthe asked.

Andreas laughed. 'No! That's for very important people.'

He knows a lot about Olympia. 'Have you been here before?' I asked.

Andreas smiled. 'Just once. A long time ago.' He pointed. 'See that olive tree by the corner of the Temple of Zeus?'

I said yes, though there were so many trees, I couldn't tell which one he meant.

'It's a sacred tree,' Andreas explained. 'Every Olympic champion has a ribbon tied round his head until the crowning ceremony.'

'They get a crown?'

Andreas laughed. 'Not a crown of gold, boy.

But, to an athlete, it's just as valuable. He's crowned with a wreath of olive leaves, cut from the sacred tree you see there.'

I didn't see it, but it would be easy to find. It'd be the one with lots of missing branches.

Andreas slipped into a doze.

'When the games start tomorrow,' I said to Chrysanthe, 'there'll be lots going on in the sports ground – all the food sellers will be down there, yum yum. There'll be lots of excitement. Pity we must stay in camp while Hilarion and your father watch the games.'

She scowled, but was quiet.

When Andreas woke, Chrysanthe jumped on his middle. 'Grandfather!'

'Ooof!' he said, laughing. 'What are you after now, little one?'

'Take me with you! To the games!'

'I've told you, Chrysanthe, the games are for men.' He rolled her off him and sat up. 'Now, don't ask again.'

That was it. Big sulk. I don't know who had the longest face over our evening meal, Chrysanthe or Hilarion. What a jolly time.

🐝 🐝 🐝

Andreas set off early today, with Hilarion fussing round him. No sign of any injury now. Well, he'll have to do his share of walking on the way home, that's for sure!

The games start with the boys' events in the morning, and chariot racing in the afternoon, then the pentathlon, which sounds exhausting. The athletes do long jump, running, wrestling and throwing the discus, then the javelin. One after the other!

I didn't see why we couldn't watch the boys' races but, if we couldn't, then at least I'd have a nice rest. Some hopes! The donkeys had a lovely time, but if only Chrysanthe had given her tongue a rest, too! She yakked from the moment Andreas and Hilarion left till the moment they came back. Play this with me, Nikoleon. Play that with me, Nikoleon. Play dollies with me, Nikoleon, or I'll tell my grandfather you were horrible to me. Take me for a walk, Nikoleon? If you don't, I'll be really upset. Let's paddle in the river, Nikoleon. Nikoleon, you beast, you're just a rotten, lazy fleabag!

She's right about the fleas, though. I've been nibbled all over today. Fleas on my legs, fleas on my arms, fleas round my neck, and a lot of fleas up my tunic. I haven't stopped scratching. It was my fault. This morning Butter settled down for a snooze in the sunshine, and I lay with my head against her warm side. The fleas must have sniffed and thought, Ha! Fresh meat!

'You can't help having fleas when you work

with donkeys,' I said sharply.

Chrysanthe laughed. 'I rode Butter all the way here, and I never got a flea on me,' she sneered.

'That's because you're not worth biting,' I said. 'You'd taste sour.'

She flounced off. Suddenly I realised she'd disappeared.

'Chrysanthe! Chrysantheeeee!'

No answer.

My stomach did flip-flops. Oh, gods, I prayed, don't let anything happen to her – Andreas would kill me. And if he did, there's not much chance of him giving my father a job.

I ran in circles, calling her. I even ran down to the edge of the little cliff and peered over, dreading I might see Chrysanthe splattered on the rocks.

There was no sign of her. I ran back to camp to find Butter missing as well. Did I forget to tether her?

No! I never forget. Chrysanthe, the little viper, had hidden from me. As soon as I went to look for her, she'd nipped back and pinched Butter.

I knew where to find her.

I mounted Twitchy, let her have a good shiver and dither, then kicked her into a reasonably fast trot and headed for the camping site.

I rode round and round, calling her, and asking if anyone had seen a child on a donkey. Nobody had.

I was in such a panic. If Andreas and Hilarion returned, what on earth would I say to them? I decided to go back to where I'd started and try to follow Butter's hoof prints. There wasn't much hope, because the ground's so hard, but it was worth trying.

Twitchy almost cantered once we'd left the camping site, then crashed through the trees to where the other donkeys were quietly grazing.

I leapt off Twitchy, and ran to where Butter

had been lying with me. That was the place to start.

Suddenly a voice screeched, 'Where on earth have you been?'

I whirled round. 'Chrysanthe! You're safe!'

'No thanks to you,' she snapped. 'You left me. I'm telling Grandfather you left me!'

I couldn't believe my ears! 'I never left you! You took Butter and ran away!'

She smirked. I swear she did.

'I was picking flowers. Butter must have got loose and followed me, but I brought her back. You should thank me for bringing her back.'

I hardly dared speak.

'Go on,' she said, 'or I'll tell Grandfather you left me. Say thank you, Fleabag.'

If Andreas thought I'd left his precious granddaughter alone, that would be the end of any exciting future for my family.

'Thank you,' I muttered.

She flounced off, calling over her shoulder,

'I'm going to ask Grandfather if I can go to the games tomorrow, and not you!'

Just then, Andreas, looking tired, trudged through the trees, leaning on Hilarion's arm. We sat him down, and Chrysanthe fetched a wine skin for him.

'Have you enjoyed the day, my dear?' he asked.

I held my breath.

'Yes, thank you, Grandfather, but it was boring with just Nikoleon for company.'

He stroked her golden hair. 'Perhaps I shouldn't have brought you,' he said. 'I just couldn't bear to be parted from you.'

She smiled, lashes fluttering over wide eyes. 'Just so we won't be parted tomorrow, ' she said, 'please may I come to the games? Just me,' she added. 'I promise to close my eyes if I see a naked man, and I'll close my ears if I hear a bad word.'

Just how she thought she could watch the games with her eyes closed, I can't imagine. But it didn't matter. I felt very satisfied seeing her face when Andreas said no.

🐝 🐝 🐝

Chrysanthe sulked practically all morning. I felt like sulking, too, because I could hear the chariot racing. I so wanted to be there. We could hear the crowd cheering and once there was an almighty groan. Maybe there was a bad crash.

It was a long, dreary day. I played dollies for hours. I had to. Chrysanthe threatened me in that silky little voice. 'If you don't, I'll tell Grandfather . . .' That was as far as I let her get. It wasn't worth arguing so, to keep the peace, I offered to make her another doll. I tied bundles of twigs with strong grasses, and wrapped moss in a piece of cloth for a head. I used a burnt twig from the fire to draw eyes and a nose on it. She was thrilled.

'Niko, you're so clever,' she cried. She's a different person when she gets her own way – a sweet little thing again.

I thought that if she had two dolls, she wouldn't need me. Stupid Niko! But I got my own back by telling her the new doll was a man. My doll ordered Zozo to stay home and cook, and not to speak until she was spoken to or he'd beat her. Every time she spoke, I made my doll grab a twig and threaten to wallop her doll.

In my mind, Zozo was Chrysanthe.

When Andreas and Hilarion came back, I couldn't wait to ask about the racing. Andreas's eyes sparkled as he told me how the horses and chariots thundered round the track, and about the falls and crashes. So exciting! Even Hilarion was slightly animated, but he soon gloomed over when Andreas told him to prepare the meal. They'd brought all sorts of good things to eat, so that cheered Chrysanthe. I made her show Andreas the doll I'd made. He patted me on the head, and said, 'Good boy.'

I just stopped myself saying, 'Woof!'

🦟 🦟 🦟

Last night, I fell asleep to the distant sounds of singing from the Olympic ground. Andreas said they were feasting and having a bit of a party, but he didn't feel up to staying.

Hilarion would have ruined it, anyway. His face would turn the wine sour.

The third day of the Olympics sounded the dullest to me – running races. One race is long, about twenty lengths of the track. But the important one is the sprint, Andreas said, and the reason it's important is that the sprint was the only race run when the Olympic games first started. I thought the crowds must have been disappointed, travelling all the way to Olympia for one little race, but it seems there weren't crowds then. Hardly anybody came. The race was run in honour of great Zeus.

Whoever wins the sprint race is considered the big star of the Olympics. Andreas was excited. 'In the morning, before the races, there'll be a great sacrifice to Zeus, of a hundred oxen,' he said.

'Ugh!' Chrysanthe shuddered.

'Where do they put the dead bodies?' I asked.

'They burn some of the bones and fat as an offering,' said Andreas, 'and the meat is cooked and shared out.'

'With everybody?' said Chrysanthe, her eyes lighting up. 'Absolutely everybody?'

Andreas laughed. 'Only those who are at the games ground,' he said. 'Don't worry, little one, I'll bring something special back to tempt you.'

Tempt her! She'd eat anything!

Chrysanthe amused herself for a while, but soon got fidgety. I was busy with my knife, trying to carve a lump of wood into an animal. Any animal would have done, but as the sun rose higher, it was clear it would only ever be a lump of wood.

Suddenly, Chrysanthe stood up. 'Turn your back.'

'No,' I said. 'That's dirty. If you need to pee, go away from the camp.'

'I don't want to pee,' she snapped. 'I want to change my clothes.'

I went to talk to the donkeys. When I returned, I couldn't believe my eyes. Chrysanthe had vanished, and a small boy was picking through our things. The cheeky little devil was already wearing my hat!

'Hoy!' I shouted. 'Push off, thief!'

The boy laughed in my face.

I darted forward and yanked my hat off his head, then stared in shock. The thieving boy was Chrysanthe! She'd changed into a shorter tunic, and had tucked her hair up underneath my hat.

'Fooled you!' she said.

'Didn't!'

She stuck out her tongue. 'Liar!'

Then she picked up a water skin. 'Come on.'

'What do you mean, come on?' I said. 'Where are you going?'

'*We* are going to the games,' she said, heading through the trees.

'Chrysanthe! Wait! What will your grandfather say when he sees you?'

'He won't!' she called back, 'You didn't recognise me, did you? So he won't.'

I quickly thrust the treasure box into the undergrowth and ran after her. 'I'll be in terrible trouble if he finds out.'

Chrysanthe plonked my hat back on her head and grinned. 'Then you'd better make sure he doesn't!'

Half of me wanted to stay, because I knew what would happen if Andreas found out I'd taken her. The other half wanted to see the games, just once. And it was the bigger half.

So we went.

We had to cross the camping site first. It was almost empty, which seemed weird, but the games ground was different altogether! Before we even reached it, we passed stalls where you could buy all sorts of things, from little pots with 'Olympic Games' written on them, to hats to protect you from the sun.

Thousands and thousands of people were ranged in front of the Temple of Zeus, watching smoke rise into the sky. The smell of roasting flesh filled my nose.

'It's the sacrifice to Zeus,' I said, and I offered up a prayer. 'Great Zeus,' I muttered, 'watch over me and help me get Andreas and everyone safely home without Chrysanthe getting me into trouble. Help Andreas to see that my father will be a good worker. And enjoy this sacrifice. It smells good.'

After the ceremony, people wandered off in all directions. We stopped to join some men watching a tame bear dancing.

'Niko,' said Chrysanthe, 'have you noticed something?'

'What?'

'It's all men here. Where are the women?'

A cheery old man turned to Chrysanthe and said, 'You'll never find a woman here, lad!'

'Why?'

'They're forbidden,' he said. 'Even women who own horses that are entered in the games – they can't watch them race.'

'I would,' said Chrysanthe, 'if they were my horses. And if I was a woman,' she added hastily. 'Which I'm not.'

The old man chuckled. 'You wouldn't come, lad – not if you were a woman. If you did, you'd be thrown over a cliff on Mount Typaeum. That's the law.'

Chrysanthe backed against me, her little body rigid.

She stared at the man. 'Not really?'

He nodded. 'Really. Tossed over, just like that. Sport's a man's world.'

Chrysanthe's hand slipped into mine. 'Niko,' she whispered. 'Let's go.'

'No,' I said. 'Let's watch a couple of races.'

'But that man . . .'

'Oh, take no notice,' I said. 'Who'd guess you're a girl? Just keep your hat on tight – my hat.'

She looked bothered, but – tough! She'd made me come, now I was going to watch a race. Then I could go home and say I really did go to the Olympic games.

We joined the spectators who sat or stood on the grassy slope overlooking the track. Lots of officials strolled around looking important.

Suddenly Chrysanthe gripped my arm. 'Look!' she squeaked. 'It's Grandfather.'

'Where?'

'Down by the starting line, on the other side

111

of the track.'

She was right. Andreas was chatting with a group of well-dressed men. Hilarion waited nearby.

An official came to the starting line and addressed the people. He rambled on about how long the Olympics had been going on, how there have been many champions in the past, and how there was one here today from long ago. All the time I was thinking, stop the yaketty-yaketty boring stuff and get on with it. But on he rambled, about how this champion here today was no ordinary champion – he'd won three competitions and yakkety yak. Then he said he was going to present him to the people.

And Andreas stepped forward!

I was stunned!

So was Chrysanthe! 'Grandfather . . . ?' she muttered. 'Grandfather?'

'Shut up!' I said. 'Just watch.'

The crowd roared for Andreas! He was

clapped on the back, and people gripped his hand, and he looked embarrassed and happy, both at the same time.

So he'd wanted to come back to Olympia, where he'd had his great triumph – and I was chosen to bring him. I felt quite important.

At that moment, I promised myself I would never again look on an elderly man as just an old dodderer. Everyone has a past – we don't know what they might have done, or what they might have been.

Chrysanthe kept saying, 'I didn't know my grandfather was famous. I didn't know.'

A great cheer went up when the athletes came to the starting line, ready for the sprint. Their bodies gleamed with oil as they jogged about, or sprang up and down, stretching their legs ready for the race.

They went to the starting line, and their bare toes curled into grooves cut into the stone.

At the cry of 'Go!' they sprang forward. At

the same time there were cries and shouts from the officials and some of the crowd. One of the athletes had started too soon.

He was dragged away by an official who thrashed him with a whip. He obviously wouldn't get another chance.

At the second attempt, the race began. The athletes hurtled the length of the running track and, right from the beginning, there was a clear winner. A thin young man, taller than the others, was way ahead and over the finishing line in what seemed no time at all. Everyone – us included – leapt up, cheering and whistling.

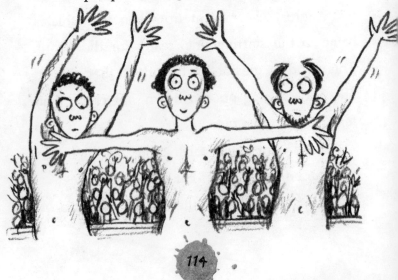

The winner had a purple ribbon tied round his head, and was acclaimed as Ariston, the Champion!

'Ohhh,' said Chrysanthe. 'No crown?'

A boy next to us said the crowns are given out at a special ceremony on the last day.

'We'll come to that, Niko,' said Chrysanthe. 'I want to see the crowning.'

'Let's wait and –' I stopped because, to my horror, I caught sight of Hilarion, on the far side of the track. He was squinting at me, and his mouth was going, but I couldn't see what he was saying.

'Quick!' I muttered. 'Hilarion's seen us. Let's go!' We slipped into the crowd and did our best to disappear. This meant trouble.

🕷 🕷 🕷

We waited in camp all afternoon. Eventually we heard footsteps coming through the trees. It was Hilarion, alone.

He dropped his packages to the ground. 'Was that you? It *was* you. Was it you?'

I couldn't deny it. I'd gone bright red.

'How could you leave Chrysanthe and the keepsake box?' he shouted.

He didn't know the 'boy' beside me had been Chrysanthe!

'When my master hears about this he'll skin you alive!' he bellowed.

Chrysanthe glanced at me. 'Grandfather doesn't know?' she asked Hilarion.

'Not yet,' he replied. 'He's been with other people all afternoon, being made a fuss of. But he will know when he gets back.'

Chrysanthe made him sit down, and knelt beside him. 'Hilarion, I've been perfectly all right. I asked Niko to go to the games, so he could tell me what it was like. I guarded the keepsake box, Niko borrowed a dog from some people he met, and the dog guarded me.'

The lies that came out of that little mouth!

'And,' she went on, 'it would be cruel to spoil Grandfather's day by telling him what Niko did.'

Hilarion scowled. 'He should be told.'

Chrysanthe looked right into his eyes. 'You're as much my slave as his. Do as I say, or I'll tell Grandfather you steal from him. Then he'll sell you.'

That did it. Hilarion sulked like mad, but he never said a word. He fed us, then, when Andreas was brought back by his new friends, he offered him food. Andreas had clearly had a lot of wine and just wanted to sleep, so no more was said.

'Thanks, Chrysanthe,' I whispered.

'It wasn't for you that I shut Hilarion up,' she

said. 'It was so we can go again tomorrow.'

Oh no!

Luckily, Andreas felt terrible this morning – all that wine, I suppose – and just wanted to sleep. There was a foul atmosphere. Chrysanthe was cross because she couldn't go to the games. Hilarion was cross because nobody was speaking to him. But me – I was just relieved there wasn't any trouble.

The afternoon was brightened by two visitors. Ariston, the new sprint champion, came with his trainer, Gregorios. He said he and Gregorios wanted to meet the man who had once won three events. They spent a long time chatting with Andreas and promised to meet at the procession before the final celebrations tomorrow. They also discovered they live near each other and will meet again in Athens.

Ariston is nice, but a bit dim. He said our mules looked very fit, and asked how hard it is to get meat to feed them on our travels. When I said

they were donkeys and they don't eat meat, he laughed and said he was joking. Oh yes?

❦ ❦ ❦

I woke today feeling glad it's the last day of the games. I'm looking forward to starting the journey home and to the end of our nerve-wracking stay here.

Andreas felt better and headed off to the games with Hilarion, who still looked as if he was sucking salt.

Once they'd left, Chrysanthe turned herself

back into a boy and said, 'You'd better disguise yourself today.'

'We're not going,' I said.

She folded her arms and tapped her foot. 'We are,' she said, 'because if we don't, I'll tell Grandfather you made me dress as a boy and go with you the other day. And you made me keep quiet. And you made Hilarion keep quiet.'

No choice, really. Off we went.

We joined the procession as it reached the front of the temple. After some dreary speeches, the first athlete stepped forward to be crowned with an olive wreath. A great cheer went up! Those with hats threw them into the air. The man next to us tossed his up, then he grabbed both mine and Chrysanthe's and threw them high.

Chrysanthe shrieked, trying to cover her golden curls with her hands. I grabbed her wrist and dragged her away. 'Run, Chrysanthe!' I shrieked. 'Run! For your life!'

People stared at the pair of us as we raced

hither and thither in the dense crowd, not knowing what direction we were going in.

Suddenly, we broke through into a clear
space. Who should be right in front of me but
Hilarion! He grabbed my arm.

'Let me go!' I yelled. 'I must get Chrysanthe
away!'

'I've got Chrysanthe,' said another voice.

It was Andreas. He looked shocked – not just
at finding us, I think, but because Chrysanthe was
hysterical.

'I don't want to die!' she screamed. 'Let me go! Please, let me go! Niko, save me! Grandfather, don't let them throw me over a cliff!'

I was crying, too. 'It's my fault. Let her go,' I begged anyone who would listen. 'Have mercy.'

Everyone ignored me.

'Hush, child,' Andreas said soothingly. 'No one shall harm you. You're safe. Hush now.'

Chrysanthe's great sobs eased. She looked up at him with tear-filled eyes. 'They won't throw me over the cliff?'

Andreas smiled, shaking his head. 'That law is for married women,' he said. 'Not helpless little girls.'

Even through a mixture of fear and relief, I found myself thinking, 'Helpless?'

Andreas got the whole story out of us, and is so angry with me he does not speak to me. Chrysanthe's upset because he's cross with her. He's livid with Hilarion for not reporting me, and cannot believe that his keepsake box hasn't been stolen, or his granddaughter kidnapped.

Personally, I blame Chrysanthe.

Whoever's to blame, everything's ruined for me and my family. I left his box unguarded. I took Chrysanthe where I shouldn't have. I let her bully me into taking her again when I knew – or at any rate, believed – she'd be in mortal danger if discovered. How could Andreas ever trust me? And if the son is not to be relied on, how could he ever imagine the father to be any better?

Tomorrow we leave.

🦑 🦑 🦑

We were packing this morning – at least, I was doing all the packing, since I was in deep disgrace – when Ariston and his trainer, Gregorios, arrived, carrying Ariston's belongings.

Gregorios is staying on at Elis for a get-together with other trainers, and asked if Ariston can travel with us. He said it would be an honour for Ariston to spend time talking with the great Andreas.

The great Andreas is delighted to have company. So delighted he's told Ariston that a victorious athlete should not walk – he should ride home in triumph.

'Hilarion will walk,' he said. 'You can ride his donkey.'

If Hilarion's face could droop any further, it did so then. 'But my ankle, master,' he whined. 'It's still weak. What shall I do?'

Andreas turned an angry eye on his slave. 'Hop!'

I led Digfoot to Ariston. 'He's a bit stubborn,' I began, but Ariston interrupted.

'I'm strong enough to handle any mu–onkey,' he said, correcting himself just in time.

I handed him the rein, then stood back, muttering, 'Hope you get on all right with your muonkey.'

Ariston mounted and dug his heels into the donkey's side. Digfoot jumped forward, then dug his hooves into the ground and off slid Ariston.

Thhlump!

I didn't laugh. Instead I helped him up. Digfoot had wandered off and now stood with his back to us.

'I'll get him,' Chrysanthe said, so I carried on loading the other donkeys. She picked a clump of grass and shook water on it, as she'd seen me do. She caught him easily. 'I'll ride him back,' she called, 'to show him he can't behave like that.' She struggled on to his back.

Ariston brushed himself down. I tied the last knot fastening Andreas's treasure box to Bolter. 'That's you done,' I said, giving the donkey a pat.

'Fine animal,' said Ariston, and instead of

giving Bolter a friendly pat, he thumped him on the rump. Bolter brayed – and bolted!

Andreas shouted, 'My box! My precious box!'

Bolter was away. He hurtled into Digfoot, but Chrysanthe held tight, then he galloped off, with the box bouncing and crashing, through the trees.

Hilarion and Ariston moved first. Andreas was shouting, 'It'll break! Catch that animal!' and Gregorios held him, saying, 'It's only a box. It'll be all right.'

Looking back, it was fate that I was slow to move because I was the only one to see what happened next. Digfoot, still prancing after being bashed into, bolted in the other direction.

Chrysanthe shrieked, 'Help!'

Andreas heard and cried in horror, 'Chrysanthe!'

Digfoot was heading down the grassy slope. I took off after him, yelling, 'Hold on!'

Chrysanthe screamed. She'd seen what I'd already thought of.

The cliff!

'Pull the reins!' I yelled, my feet pounding along. My heart thundered in my ears.

Suddenly Digfoot saw what was ahead. He lived up to his name, and dug his feet in, hard. Chrysanthe shot over the top, just where the slope grew steeper.

She started to roll! I don't know how I did it, but I put on a spurt and just as it seemed she'd go over the cliff, I threw myself flat and grabbed her by the ankle.

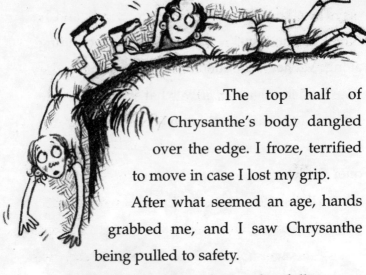

The top half of Chrysanthe's body dangled over the edge. I froze, terrified to move in case I lost my grip.

After what seemed an age, hands grabbed me, and I saw Chrysanthe being pulled to safety.

Now, I'm lying by a fire, with a full tummy. Andreas is cradling sleepy Chrysanthe in his arms. Hilarion is dozing. Ariston and Gregorios are talking quietly. Everyone was too shaken up to start travelling today, and I had to see to some cuts on Bolter's side and legs.

We're leaving tomorrow. I'll be glad to get home.

🐜 🐜 🐜

What a day!

Before we left, Gregorios spoke to me. He

says he's been a trainer for many years, and he knows a good athlete when he sees one.

'Nikoleon,' he said, 'I saw you run yesterday. You could become an athlete.'

'Me?' I said. 'But I never run anywhere.'

'You walk!' he said. 'Those legs are strong, and have much power in them. If you work hard, you will be a great athlete. Can you work hard?'

'Er, what do you mean – work hard?' I asked.

'I'm saying,' said Gregorios, 'that when we get back to Athens, I would like you to join my gymnasium and begin training.'

I blew my cheeks out. 'By the gods,' I said, 'that would be a wonderful thing. Me, a great athlete! Wouldn't my family be proud.'

Thoughts of my family made me see sense. 'No, I can't join your gymnasium,' I said. 'I have to work for my father. You see our farm isn't –'

Ariston giggled. Gregorios put up a hand to shut me up. 'Andreas has something to say about that.'

I turned. Andreas stood with his hands on Chrysanthe's shoulders. 'Nikoleon,' he said. 'There was I shouting after my keepsake box, while you ran to save Chrysanthe – the most precious thing in the world to me. I'd rather the box were smashed to bits than let a hair of this child's head be damaged.' He smiled. 'Niko, you will go to the gymnasium. Your father will work for me and, if he is honest and true, your family will never want for anything. That will be your reward.'

I still can't believe he said that! Even Hilarion was nice to me. 'If Chrysanthe had been killed,' he said, 'my master would have died of a broken heart. I'd have been sold, and would have to leave my home.'

I took advantage of his friendliness (it probably

won't last) and asked, 'What is in the treasure box? What might have broken?'

'A painted vase,' said Hilarion.

'A vase! Why was that so precious?'

'It was presented to Andreas when the city of Athens honoured him for his triumph at the Olympic games,' said Hilarion. 'And it did break.'

Blow Bolter and stupid Ariston. 'Is Andreas dreadfully upset?' I asked.

'He was at first,' said Hilarion. 'But then he realised that the true treasure, though it's old and brittle and faded now, is the wreath that crowned Andreas as the champion of the Olympic games. That can never be replaced, but it is safe.'

Chrysanthe was tickling Butter's nose with a pink flower. Hilarion's wrong, I thought. Chrysanthe – not the wreath – is his true treasure.

I gave the donkeys water, and checked their halters to make sure nothing rubbed. I was a bit clumsy – Nipper bit me, Digfoot stamped when I touched him, and Twitchy quivered and shivered

and danced away from me. It was as if, all of a sudden, they didn't know me!

Now we're on our way. Grandmother said I need bring nothing back, just myself, and if the gods grant her prayer, I will do so. But she doesn't know that I'm bringing much more than that. I'm bringing the promise of a bright future for myself and my family.

I'm even bringing a souvenir of my Olympian journey – my own vase! We stopped at the potter's home on the way back, and he gave me the one I painted. It's been fired, and it's beautiful. I won't be peeing in it!

All I need do now is get this lot home safely.

I hope I can – I feel really odd. Not myself at all.

Shame I've got to walk. Still – it's good for the legs! Just have to keep dodging the donkey doo . . .

Toby straightened up. 'Woah!' he said. 'Must have dropped off. Glad Hilarion let me have a ride in the end.' He rubbed his eyes, still feeling a bit peculiar, then looked round at his own fairy-decorated room. 'Oh! I'm me again.'

Before he could think another thought, the door flew open. 'Toby! I've been calling you,' said Evie. She grinned. 'Playing horses?'

Toby realised he was sitting astride the wooden chest.

'Course not,' he said crossly.

'Only joking,' she said. 'Can you turn that racket down a bit, please?' She nodded towards the CD player.

Toby got off the chest and reached for the controls.

'Well, don't just stare at it, turn it down,' said Evie. 'I'm making drinks if you fancy hot chocolate.' She glanced at the pile of paper scraps. 'Been working on your family tree?'

Toby didn't hear her. He'd put that CD on when he began doing the family tree. It was still playing, yet he'd been to Olympia. Well, Niko had been to Olympia.

Evie shrugged and left. Toby felt shaky, and sat on the floor, looking at the wooden chest. He'd actually become Nikoleon – his own ancestor. Niko was part of his family tree. And the chest was full of names. Full of secrets.

He picked up the bat and, not really concentrating, began hitting the ball against the wall.

'The chest did its magic again. I was Nikoleon,' he said, whacking the ball over and over. 'OK, let's see. Who's Toby Tucker? Toby Tucker has Egyptian blood, and he has a Greek ancestor who might have been a famous Olympic champion.'

He carried on idly hitting the ball.

Don bounded upstairs. 'That racket's worse than the music,' he said. 'What are you doing? Jumping off the wardrobe?'

'Look, Don!' Toby said, excitedly. 'I couldn't do it before, but I've been doing it over and over again, and now I can!'

'Can what?'

'Hit the fairy right on the nose,' said

Toby. 'Every time, look!' He laughed. 'I'm going to keep practising till I beat you at table tennis!'

'No chance!' said Don.

'You can do anything if you keep trying,' said Toby, thinking of how he'd put up with Chrysanthe for so long, all for the sake of his – Niko's – family. 'And if you want something badly enough.'

'Then why don't we go for a run round the park?' said Don. 'Get you in shape for the next sports day trials.' He eyed Toby's newish trainers. 'Better change your shoes. You don't want to tread in something nasty in those.'

Toby laughed. 'Don't worry! I'm used to that!'

As they left, he glanced at the chest and thought with longing, 'Next time!'

Who will TOBY TUCKER be next?

He's Seti, keeping sneaky secrets in Ancient Egypt!

He's Titus, sludging through the sewer in Ancient Rome!

He's John Bunn, mucking about with monkeys in Tudor London!

He's Alfie Trott, picking people's pockets in Victorian London!

He's Fred Barrow, hogging all the pig swill in wartime London!

EGMONT PRESS: ETHICAL PUBLISHING

Egmont Press is about turning writers into successful authors and children into passionate readers – producing books that enrich and entertain. As a responsible children's publisher, we go even further, considering the world in which our consumers are growing up.

Safety First
Naturally, all of our books meet legal safety requirements. But we go further than this; every book with play value is tested to the highest standards – if it fails, it's back to the drawing-board.

Made Fairly
We are working to ensure that the workers involved in our supply chain – the people that make our books – are treated with fairness and respect.

Responsible Forestry
We are committed to ensuring all our papers come from environmentally and socially responsible forest sources.

For more information, please visit our website at
www.egmont.co.uk/ethicalpublishing